Howe Library

Hanover, NH

BY LEDA SCHUBERT

NATHAN'S SONG

PICTURES BY MAYA ISH-SHALOM

 DIAL BOOKS FOR YOUNG READERS

For my wonderful
Broffman/Lerman family
—L.S.

For Natan and Alma
—M.I.S.

DIAL BOOKS FOR YOUNG READERS
An imprint of Penguin Random House LLC · New York

First published in the United States of America by Dial Books for Young Readers,
an imprint of Penguin Random House LLC, 2021

Text copyright © 2021 by Leda Schubert
Illustrations copyright © 2021 by Maya Ish-Shalom

Visit us online at penguinrandomhouse.com.
Dial and colophon are registered trademarks of Penguin Random House LLC.

Library of Congress Cataloging-in-Publication Data is available.

The artwork for this book was created digitally.
Design by Jason Henry · Printed in China
ISBN 9781984815781 · 10 9 8 7 6 5 4 3 2 1

From the time Nathan was a little boy in Russia, he loved to sing. He sang when he stacked wood, he sang when he peeled potatoes, and he sang when he fetched water from the well.

"That Nathan!" said the neighbors. "He can lift your heart with his voice."

Everyone in Nathan's shtetl taught him their favorite songs, and he sang them all.

One day a famous opera singer gave a concert in the next village. Nathan and his family were there.

"I did not know anything could be so beautiful," said Nathan. "I want to sing like that."

"Then you must study in Italy," Papa said. "The best teachers are there."

"But how can I go?" Nathan said. "We have no money!"

"We will find a way," said Mama.

For many months Nathan did extra chores for the neighbors. His parents scrimped and saved, and family and friends gave what they could. Even his little brother, Samuel, helped.

On Nathan's sixteenth birthday, Mama said, "It is time. We have enough for you to travel." Her handkerchief was wet with tears.

"How will I ever see you again?" Nathan asked.

"When you become a famous singer, send for us and we will come," said Papa.

"I promise."

Nathan packed a cloth bag and tied his coins in a
pouch around his waist. Such sobbing and hugging!
Samuel followed Nathan through the village.

"Here, Samuel. Keep my cap for me."

"Only until I see you again," Samuel said.

Nathan traveled on foot, on horseback, and by cart for many weeks, singing to keep himself going.

He finally reached the Black Sea, and after he purchased his ticket, he wandered the waterfront looking for his ship.

"Can you show me the dock for Italy?" Nathan asked over
and over, but no one bothered to answer. The port was crowded,
and the shouting and clanging hurt his ears. The names on the
ships were in many different languages. Nathan was so tired,
his eyes were blurry. When he found a Russian ship,
he climbed the gangplank, leaving his home forever.

The land became a distant speck and a sailor said,

NEXT STOP, NEW YORK!

"New York?" Nathan cried. "But my ticket is for Italy!"

The sailor hailed the captain. "This boy is on the wrong ship."

"Well, boy," said the captain. "Should we throw you overboard?"

"I can sing for my supper," Nathan said.

"Let's see how you do," said the captain.

Nathan smiled for the first time since leaving home.

Sing he did, at the glittering captain's table during the
fancy dinners, at the dances for the ladies and gentlemen
with their diamonds, and even for the crowded passengers
in steerage.

When the ship docked in New York, the captain said,
"You more than earned your passage. Here is money
to help you eat."

The buildings in New York hid the sky. Horses whinnied, people yelled, and even the smells were strange. *There is only one thing I can do,* Nathan thought. On busy street corners, he sang. Strangers threw coins into his basket.

He rented a tiny room and learned English, but every night he missed his family more. In his letters he told them how much he loved them, and he told them about America.

Nathan found a job making and selling hats. While he worked, there was always music in his head. Opera music—the music he yearned to sing.

On the streets, the listening crowds swelled.

In summer, a man came up to him and said, "You have a voice in a million, but it needs training. May I teach you?"

"I cannot afford to pay you," Nathan said.

"Don't worry. I would like to have a student like you. I am Nicolo."

Nathan and Nicolo studied together every night, and Nathan worked very hard as the weeks and months passed. His voice grew richer and sweeter. At night his song drifted over the city.

After a year, Nicolo said, "Now we are ready to put you to work." So Nathan sang his beloved opera in restaurants, and at weddings, and even in small theaters.

Then, on one exciting night, he joined performers on a big Broadway stage.

People clapped wildly. "That Nathan, he's the best," they said, and offered him more work.

But Nathan's fame did not fill the loneliness in his heart.
He saved and saved, and finally he mailed three tickets for
the ocean passage to his family in the shtetl.
He waited and waited.

Some Russian girls came into the hat shop. One had laughing eyes, and Nathan couldn't help speaking to her. "My name is Sonia," she told him in Yiddish. She returned the next day, alone. Nathan invited her out for a cup of tea.

When they parted, he sang her an old love song, and before he finished, she took his hand.

Three months later, Nathan and Sonia were married. There was plenty of dancing and eating and, of course, Nathan sang. The bride and groom were lifted high in the air on chairs when, in the back of the crowd, Nathan thought he saw his old cap.

He sang out, "Samuel. Is it really you?"

"I am here!" Samuel said.

"But where are Mama and Papa?"

Samuel smiled. "They will come soon.

First, we'll find a home for all of us together."

Nathan found an apartment with enough room for everyone. He mailed a letter.

A few months later he, Sonia, and Samuel journeyed to Ellis Island.

"There are so many people," Sonia said.
"How will we ever find them?"

Nathan knew. He sang, and his powerful voice rose
over the crowds. He sang with all the love he had.

Mama and Papa heard and came running.

"This is my wife, Sonia," Nathan said.

"We are happy to meet you," said Papa, shaking hands.

Mama just put her arms around Sonia and said,

"Call me Mama."

The great hall seemed full of music, Russia, and New York,
and Nathan's life was full of family again. At last.

AUTHOR'S NOTE

This story was inspired by my grandfather, who was born during the final decade of the nineteenth century in what was then Bessarabia, a part of Russia. Life for Jews in Russia was extremely challenging. Most were forced to live in a restricted area known as "The Pale," were rarely allowed to own land, and were subject to frequent pogroms (massacres) and other anti-Semitic actions. They could only work in limited professions. For these and other reasons, millions of Jews left Russia before World War I. Among them were my grandparents and their families.

Like many immigrants today, one member of a family frequently left for America first. He or she worked hard to accumulate enough money to send for other family members, one by one. My grandmother Sonia was the third from her family to arrive in New York, leaving Russia and everything she knew when she was about thirteen years old.

My grandfather Nathan (or Nat) left home when he was about twenty. He had a magnificent baritone voice and planned to study opera in Italy, but he somehow boarded the wrong ship and ended up in Brazil. He sold clothing and hats from a pushcart for a few years until he could afford a ticket to New York. There, he met Sonia in a park and fell in love.

Sonia and Nat had two children, my mother (Edith) and my uncle (Morton). Sonia worked for a time in the Triangle Shirtwaist Factory, a few years after the infamous fire that killed 123 women and 23 men. Nathan worked making hats.

But he continued to sing and performed in three Broadway musicals: *The Desert Song*, *East Wind*, and *Princess Flavia*. He also was featured on several New York radio shows. Best of all, he could almost always be persuaded to sing at our family gatherings, usually in Russian. I will never forget his beautiful voice.